Author's note

Use this book interactively! Take your time to explore each pose and notice how your body feels. There's no "right" way to do these yoga-inspired postures. The goal is to help you get out of your head and into your body. When you connect your body and breath, you become more present and calm, which helps you flow more easily with life's ups and downs.

Breathe along with this book! When breathing is cued, pause reading to take some breaths. Play with slowly breathing in through your nose and out through your mouth. Try letting out a big sigh like a fiery dragon. Slowing down your breath can help slow down your mind.

I hope this book feels like a breath of fresh air as you breathe, move, and bend with your animal friends!

Hands to Heart

by Alex Bauermeister
Illustrated by Flora Waycott

Houghton Mifflin Harcourt
Boston New York

For my daughter Aviva —A. B.

For Shima the cat, who endlessly inspires —F. W.

Settle in, my friend.
It's time to start.
So take a big breath.
Bring your hands to your heart.

Whether your breath
is flowing fast or slow.

Whether your mood is
soaring high or low.

By moving and breathing
you can calm your mind.
The whole world gets clearer—
let's see what we find.

Here we go now.
Lift your arms,
reach high!

Take some big breaths.
Can you breathe
to the sky?

Let's move our arms
like we're swimming
through air.

Try it fast, try it slow.
You can add your own flair!

Now let's give
ourselves a great big hug.
Wrap your arms around you.
Breathe slow and hold snug.

Let's pose like a cat
on hands and knees.
Stretch your back and your shoulders.

Move around as you please!

Now let's pose like a cow.
Drop your belly real low.
Arch your back, lift your tail.

Now breathe real slow.

What happens when we mix
the cat and the cow?

Drop your belly, breathe in.

Round your back,
breathe out now.

Now let's make like a dog.
Are you ready to shift?
Press your paws to the floor.
Let your whole body lift.

Stretch your hips up and back.
Downward dog is the pose.
Let your head hang low.
Slowly breathe through your nose.

Now seems like a good time
to lie on the floor.
Lie down on your belly.
Breathe here once more.

Stretch your legs long behind you
like a cobra snake!
Lift and lower your chest.
Cobra is sleeping—then awake.

Roll onto your back.
Let your shoulders rest.

Next, bend your knees.
Hug them close to your chest.

It’s time for a twist.
Reach your arms out wide.

Breathing real slow,
sway your legs side to side.

Let your eyes get heavy.
Bring your hands to your heart.
Rest your legs,
thank your body!
Each limb did its part.

Next time your mind
needs a moment of rest,
breathe slow, stretch your body.
It's your heart that knows best.

Alex Bauermeister

is a yoga therapist helping people find more authenticity, courage, and connection in their lives. She used to work from behind a desk to change policy and organizations; now she works from the mat to help people change themselves through yoga and mindfulness. Alex has a business degree and specializes in Phoenix Rising Yoga Therapy and Kripalu Yoga, as well as leadership training in social justice and anti-racism work. Her writing was chiefly inspired by her toddler, who loves to climb on her while in child's pose and is just learning the messy art of self-regulation. She lives in Boston with her family. This is her picture book debut.

intrayogatherapy.com

Flora Waycott

is an illustrator from the South of England, currently based in Sydney, Australia. She works both digitally and traditionally, with her illustrations appearing on book covers, children's bedding and decor, stationery, greeting cards, coloring books, and more. She is also inspired by everyday objects—from the contents of her kitchen cupboard to travel and adventure in faraway places.

florawaycott.com